2007
Mini Saga Competition

Young Writers

in association with

STAEDTLER

# mini
# S·A·G·A·S·

## Fife

First published in Great Britain in 2008 by
Young Writers, Remus House, Coltsfoot Drive,
Peterborough, PE2 9JX
Tel (01733) 890066 Fax (01733) 313524
All Rights Reserved

# Foreword

Young Writers was established in 1991, with the aim of encouraging the children and young adults of today to think and write creatively. Our latest secondary school competition, 'Mini S.A.G.A.S.', posed an exciting challenge for these young authors: to write, in no more than fifty words, a story encompassing a beginning, a middle and an end. We call this the mini saga.

Mini S.A.G.A.S. *Fife* is our latest offering from the wealth of young talent that has mastered this incredibly challenging form. With such an abundance of imagination, humour and ability evident in such a wide variety of stories, these young writers cannot fail to enthral and excite with every tale.

# Contents

**Dunfermline High School**

Teighan Brown (12) ............................ 11
Emily Christie (12) ............................ 12
Emma Clyne (12) .............................. 13
Ellen Cree (14) ................................ 14
Sean Horder (12) .............................. 15
Sally Ann Lamond (12) ........................ 16
Kier McCallum (12) ........................... 17
Sally Melville (12) ............................. 18
Catriona Murphy (12) ......................... 19
Rebecca Neilson (12) ......................... 20
Susan Simpson (12) ........................... 21
Ryan Thompson (11) .......................... 22
Rachel Williamson (12) ....................... 23
Hannah Anderson (14) ........................ 24
Aileen Baxter (14) ............................ 25
Lewis Bogue (14) .............................. 26
Emma Bullock (14) ............................ 27
Andy Christie (14) ............................ 28
Hayley Cook (14) .............................. 29
Dale Cuthbertson (14) ........................ 30
Fiona Dawson (14) ............................ 31
Abby Hynd (14) ............................... 32
Louise Jenkins (14) ........................... 33
Rachel McDonald (14) ........................ 34

Ashleigh MacQueen (14) ..................... 35
Robbie Michie (14) ........................... 36
Katie Reid (14) ............................... 37
Cameron Renwick (14) ....................... 38
Emma Thomson (14) .......................... 39
Alyssa Watson (14) ........................... 40
Duncan Austin (11) ........................... 41
Mhairi Clark (12) ............................. 42
Emma Cockburn (12) ......................... 43
Aimee Easton (12) ............................ 44
Laura Joyce (12) .............................. 45
Joeanne Nicol (12) ........................... 46
Erin Paterson (12) ............................ 47
Andrew Sherriffs (12) ........................ 48
Lauren Turnbull (12) ......................... 49
Esmé Wilkinson (11) .......................... 50

**Falkland House School**

Anton Zarzoso (11) ........................... 51
Joshua Gracie (14) ........................... 52
Jonathan Burke (12) .......................... 53
Steven Barrett (14) ........................... 54
Oliver Costigan (10) .......................... 55
Ross Hogg (14) ............................... 56
Ryan Brotherston (13) ........................ 57
Liam Louden (14) ............................. 58

## Kirkland High School & Community College

Amy Graham (13) ............................................. 59
Steven Robertson (13) ................................... 60
Alex Adams (13) ............................................. 61
Robbie Leitch (13) ......................................... 62
Kelsey Wilson (13) ......................................... 63
Nicola England (13) ....................................... 64
Ross Macfarlane (13) ..................................... 65
Sarah Bradley (13) ......................................... 66
Steven Welsh (12) ......................................... 67
Baillie Blount (13) ......................................... 68
Niall Anderson (13) ....................................... 69

## St Leonard's School, St Andrews

Flora Ogilvy (13) ........................................... 70
Dominique Haferkamp (15) ........................... 71
Lily Watts (13) .............................................. 72
Rebecca Taylor (13) ...................................... 73
Olivia Collison-Owen (13) ............................ 74
Grace Collison-Owen (13) ............................ 75
Jamie Hartley (13) ......................................... 76
Claudia Beasley (13) ..................................... 77
Callum Robertson (13) .................................. 78
Olivia Cassidy (13) ........................................ 79
Natalie Degroot (13) ..................................... 80
Anna Rolland (13) ......................................... 81
Ian Redford (15) ........................................... 82
Ewan Anderson (12) ..................................... 83
Claire Marston (11) ...................................... 84
Miriam Balfour (12) ...................................... 85
Mikayla Head (12) ......................................... 86
Lauren Goadby (11) ...................................... 87
Charlotte Fitton (12) .................................... 88
Michael Overend (13) ................................... 89
Lauren Sandeman (14) ................................... 90
Liam Deboys (15) .......................................... 91
Rebecca Mansbridge (14) .............................. 92
Annabel Zajicek (13) ..................................... 93
Joseph Levett (15) ........................................ 94
Fiona Baird (13) ............................................ 95
Josh Jamieson (14) ........................................ 96
Ged Rutherford (13) ..................................... 97
Darya Vinogradov-Wouters (12) ..................... 98

## Woodmill High School

Aime Allan (12) ............................................. 99
Emma Archer (13) ......................................... 100
Sophie Balsillie (12) ...................................... 101
Christopher Bogie (12) .................................. 102
Kelly Boniface (13) ........................................ 103
Jonathan Cameron (13) .................................. 104
Nicole Chappell (12) ..................................... 105
Tiffany Concannon (13) .................................. 106
Megan Doran (12) ......................................... 107
Aaron Dougan (14) ........................................ 108
Carla Dow (13) ............................................. 109
Hannah Fell (12) ........................................... 110
Benjamin Folan (13) ...................................... 111

Michael Henderson (13) .................................. 112
Daniel Jones (12) ............................................. 113
Ryan Kay (13) .................................................. 114
Kerry Keilloh (13) ........................................... 115
Christopher Leslie (11) ................................... 116
Stewart McDonald (12) .................................. 117
Kendra McPherson (12) ................................. 118
Kirsty-Marie Moran (13) ................................ 119
Lauren Queen (13) .......................................... 120
Nisha Rach (13) ............................................... 121
Chlöe Reilly (13) ............................................. 122
Tomas Mark Sibbald (12) ............................... 123
Conor Smith (12) ............................................ 124
Vicky Sparling (13) .......................................... 125
Craig Stephen (12) .......................................... 126
Cameron Tasker (12) ...................................... 127
Sean Tetsall (13) ............................................. 128
Fearghas Urquhart (11) ................................... 129
Samantha McDonald (12) ............................... 130
Tony McAulay (14) .......................................... 131
Ashleigh McAndrew (12) ................................ 132
Gemma Lane (13) ............................................ 133
Adam Gillen (13) ............................................. 134
Sara Eydmann (12) .......................................... 135
Maddie Coussens (13) ..................................... 136
Lauren Buchanan (13) ..................................... 137
Robyn Allan (13) ............................................. 138

# The Mini Sagas

# The Visit

'Daddy, what are you doing?' I asked.
'Why are you doing Santa's job?'
'What? Em … well em, I'm not your dad
little girl, I'm Santa,' he said alarmed.
I ran upstairs and my dad was fast asleep.
I ran back down, but he was gone.
'Santa?' I said, amazed.

**Teighan Brown (12)**
**Dunfermline High School**

# The Abyss

Tears stream down my bloodstained face.
My hair is plastered to my face. I scream, feeling
something touch my foot. Despair, black and terrifyingly
delicious washes over me. Someone's watching me.
I feel their gaze and hear laughter. I feel searing pain
clasp me. I slip into never-ending darkness.

**Emily Christie (12)**
**Dunfermline High School**

12

# Surprising Sleepover

She needs a haircut. Not anything
too drastic. I gathered my Barbies together.
*Just do it*, said the voices in my head. My friend
was asleep. *Snip, snip!* The next thing I heard
was a shrill scream to be heard miles away.
'I thought you needed one too!' I exclaimed.

**Emma Clyne (12)**
**Dunfermline High School**

# Sledging

I stepped into the bitter coldness.
Walking down the path, footprints following
me on my way. Up the hill I looked to the white,
sparkling blanket below. Suddenly, I was zooming
down. I felt I could fly! The wind caught my breath.
I'd been sledging for the first time.

**Effen Cree (12)**
**Dunfermline High School**

# Waiting

The clock ticked away. I lay still.
The tension was unbearable. I watched
the clock beside me, counting the minutes.
Waiting is harder and longer when you actually do it.
I knew what was coming, I just wanted to explode.
Thoughts were rushing through my head.
I'm waiting for Christmas!

**Sean Horder (12)**
**Dunfermline High School**

# Falling

Sunlight beat against the back of my neck.
Desert wind whipped my hair into a wild, furious
flame. I was desperate to escape. Stretching out to
a ledge, my foot felt the rock crumble to dust
beneath me. Guards came closer. My body jerked
backwards violently. Falling. It was over!

**Saffy Ann Lamond (12)**
**Dunfermline High School**

# The Chase

I am speeding down the road 100mph. The police are right on my tail. This makes me speed up. *Crash!* I hit the back of another car. My engine catches fire. *Bang!* It blows up into hundreds of pieces. I'm dead. Oh well, I'd better restart the game then!

**Kier McCallum (12)**
**Dunfermline High School**

# Debut Single

Thousands of eyes followed me as I crept
on stage. I threw back my head and sang a long,
harmonious note. Anticipation gripped the nation.
The bass line roared and the drums beat heavily
down. Everyone agreed afterwards that it
was the best rock concert in town.

**Saffy Melville (12)**
**Dunfermline High School**

18

# On Top Of The World

It was pitch-black as I climbed the mammoth mountain, my feet slipping out from under me. Fear raced through my body as I reached the top. Suddenly, I fell all the way down to my bed and the mountain of washing was defeated.

**Catriona Murphy (12)**
**Dunfermline High School**

# Tig

Darkness was closing in around me.
I was running as fast as I could. My eyes watering,
sweat pouring down my face, he was behind me.
I couldn't stop. I could only think of the pain.
*Thud!* I landed on the ground. It was over.
My brother's voice, 'You're it!'

**Rebecca Neilson (12)**
**Dunfermline High School**

# Cliff-Hanger

The sun was shining in the air. With fear in my eyes as I was stopped at the top counting from 10 to 1, as I waited to be dropped from 100 feet. I suddenly fell, screaming all the way down and then I touched the ground off cliff-hanger.

**Susan Simpson (12)**
**Dunfermline High School**

# The Secret Santa

I walked downstairs in the middle of the night and I got a terrible fright. For there stood a man all dressed in red with a funny little hat on his head. He looked at me, put his finger to his lip and said, 'Merry Christmas, little boy.'

**Ryan Thompson (11)**
**Dunfermline High School**

# Graveyard

There I was, in the middle of this old, creepy graveyard amidst row upon row of old, cracked, moss-covered stones. I stood rooted to the spot. I took a deep breath. The dark figure moved towards me. I ran and tripped. He loomed over me …
I screamed and awoke!

**Rachel Williamson (12)**
**Dunfermline High School**

23

# Untitled

I ran as fast as I could, the wind and rain
hitting my face. I was too scared to look back in
case it was behind me. I ran into the alley in search
of a place to hide. I crouched down behind
a bin, but then it grabbed me …

**Hannah Anderson (14)**
**Dunfermline High School**

# Bloodthirsty

Huddling in the corner, I heard the door creak open and then a satisfied grunt from the bloodthirsty beast that wanted to take my life. Eyes meeting mine, it rushed toward me, mouth wide open. Canines penetrated into my eyes. Blood trickled down my face.

**Aileen Baxter (14)**
**Dunfermline High School**

# Abandoned

Myself and my thoughts were the only things left in the abandoned copse. There was nowhere to go. Nothing but loneliness in my thoughts. The only thing left to keep me occupied was the droplet of water seeping from the cavern wall.

**Lewis Bogue (14)**
**Dunfermline High School**

# Running From Darkness

I could hear footsteps and faint whistling
noises coming nearer behind me as branches and
leaves brushed roughly against my face. The darkness
didn't help the fear I was feeling and I felt the wind as
tense as I felt my heartbeat. Then, from nothing,
I saw distant bright light …

**Emma Bullock (14)**
**Dunfermline High School**

27

# The Chase

My brother and I were being chased.
Mark ran ahead. I got caught and was put into a log
on a conveyor belt. Ahead were these spinning,
sharp-edged discs. It was shredding the log. It hit
me and then there was darkness. I woke up
screaming my brother's name.

**Andy Christie (14)**
**Dunfermline High School**

# Hide-And-Seek

Trembling with fear, time seemed frozen.
I sat rocking under the old, wrecked bed. Footsteps
grew louder, then we heard the screech of the door
handle and his cold, terrifying voice growing louder.
We held our breath as he crouched to the floor.
He came to his knees:
'Found you!'

**Hayley Cook  (14)**
**Dunfermline High School**

# Polar Escape

I felt the frosty crunch beneath my feet.
Winter should be ending soon, but it was still frosty
and cold. I took a run towards the lake surface. I hit
the water with a crack. I tried to scream but
the freezing water froze inside my lungs.

**Dale Cuthbertson (14)**
**Dunfermline High School**

# The Drop

My heart pounded as if about to leap out my chest. The butterflies in my stomach became a sort of hiccupping feeling. The tall, dark figure beside me stared daringly into my eyes as a rope was tied tightly around my neck. I stepped forward and then the drumming stopped …

**Fiona Dawson (14)**
**Dunfermline High School**

# That Night Was Different

It was midnight, scared as I ran through
the night knowing I was being chased by that thing.
Suddenly, the footsteps behind me stopped. I took
a chance to look. There was nothing there. Turning
round again, something grabbed my shoulder.
I turned my head … it was him! *Oh no!*

### Abby Hynd (14)
**Dunfermline High School**

32

# Death By Religion

As the plane neared the building, my heart was racing. I couldn't believe I was doing this for my religion. Doors were banging as the outraged passengers found out. The plane, going at the speed of light, my heart still pounding, I pressed the dreaded button. The deed was done.

**Louise Jenkins (14)**
**Dunfermline High School**

33

# Home Sweet Home

I was blown backwards by the force of the explosion.
I lay face down in the mud, hoping the shrapnel
would miss me. Slowly, I crawled silently through
the darkness, back to my trench, to the place I call
'home', to the place that would be the death of me.

**Rachel McDonald (14)**
**Dunfermline High School**

34

# A Walk In The Woods

A young boy went out for a walk in the park and came across a huge ditch. When he looked into it, he saw an alien. When he started to run away, it came out of the ditch and tried to shoot him. He managed to get away …

**Ashleigh MacQueen (14)**
**Dunfermline High School**

# The Crater Of Europe

It was the year 2090 and Skott was with his parents in outer space, watching the crater of Europe fill with molten lava. Another spaceship collided with his parents' ship. From the safety of his own ship, Skott watched his parents fall into the crater, disappearing into the boiling lava.

**Robbie Michie (14)**
**Dunfermline High School**

# The Stage

I closed my eyes as the curtain rose. The sheer volume of the crowd was overwhelming. I opened my eyes to a crowd, thousands of people all anxious to see me. Children of all ages screaming my name. This is what I live for, this is where I'm home.

**Katie Reid (14)**
**Dunfermline High School**

# The End

They reached the cemetery. They usually stopped and turned back at this point. Not tonight though. They dared themselves to continue. A scream! Matt dropped to the ground, unconscious. The others petrified, sweat dripping off their faces. What was going on? All they knew was that this was the end.

**Cameron Renwick (14)**
**Dunfermline High School**

# My New Laptop

It was Christmas Day so I got up and went downstairs as fast as I could. I looked at all the presents under the tree. There were lots, but that was when I saw it, my new laptop. It was the best day of my life. I was so excited.

**Emma Thomson (14)**
**Dunfermline High School**

# Untitled

The footsteps grew louder as they
approached my front door. My heart pounded faster.
I could now make out their faces. Blood dripped
from their fang-like teeth. *Knock, knock.* I had to
be brave. Trembling, I opened the front door.
I watched their vicious mouths opening,
'Trick or treat?'

**Alyssa Watson (14)**
**Dunfermline High School**

# Feeding Time

The lion creeps closer. *Pad, pad, pad,* go his feet on the grass, almost as if he can see me. He's drooling in anticipation of a good kill. Now I'm incredibly petrified. He's tensing his body, preparing to pounce …
'We'll be back after a short interval,' boomed the television presenter.

**Duncan Austin (11)**
**Dunfermline High School**

# The Greens

I surrender to all evil and destruction.
Please, I will give in really. Oh no, my life is over.
The catastrophe, the pain of it all. I was as wobbly as
some jelly. I'll eat the Brussels sprouts. What have I
done? Can I not just leave one? Why not?

**Mhairi Clark (12)**
**Dunfermline High School**

# New Class

My head was pounding, my palms were sweating as I marched down the elongated hallway. The voices around me were drowned out by my thumping heart and the dazzling colours and numbers around me were a blur. Suddenly, a door swung open and I stepped into my new, dazzling classroom.

**Emma Cockburn (12)**
**Dunfermline High School**

# Brace Free!

As my mum and I walked into the orthodontist's room, Mum reassured me that getting braces off would not be extremely painful. When I had clambered into the chair, nerves really took over me. As my orthodontist was finishing, I realised it hadn't been that sore! Now I'm brace free!

**Aimee Easton (12)**
**Dunfermline High School**

44

# Untitled

I was shivering, couldn't move as a shadow peered round the corner. All I knew was he was standing behind me with a gun in his hand. I was too scared to cry. Then he pulled the trigger and I let out a loud shriek.
Then I woke up!

**Laura Joyce (12)**
**Dunfermline High School**

# Drowning

As I struggled and squirmed, I found myself looking at darkness. I couldn't breathe, some force was stopping me. I could hear voices screaming and shouting. I found the bottom, I pushed. I could see light emerging. Taking a breath I found myself above the water at a swimming pool.

**Joeanne Nicol (12)**
**Dunfermline High School**

# Shiny, Sparkly And Dazzling

Wow! It's colossal! Pure, shiny emerald and real gold. The diamonds and sparkly jewels make it glow like the night sky. My sister's eyes glitter as she stares at it in amazement. The creamy chocolate hangs from its branches, light as feathers! I've never seen such a dazzling Christmas tree!

**Erin Paterson (12)**
**Dunfermline High School**

# Fireworks

*Boom! Bang!* My heart felt like it was going to explode with excitement. There goes another one rushing into the black ocean of night. *Bang! Boom!* I gave out a massive cry like my lungs were trying to escape. All of a sudden, silence. The fireworks had stopped. Not good!

**Andrew Sherriffs (12)**
**Dunfermline High School**

# The Real World

He crept up behind him. I tried to shout, but I couldn't.
He crept up closer. I couldn't help myself. I screamed.
I kept on screaming until he turned around. Suddenly:
'Shut up, we're trying to watch a film here!' The men
and women behind me shouted angrily.

**Lauren Turnbull (12)**
**Dunfermline High School**

# The Race

A flash of light, scream of sound. The cold rushing through my body. Soon my muscles ached and my head was spinning, but it didn't matter. As I smacked the wall with two hands, the click of timer's hands in the air. I had done it. The trophy was mine.

**Esmé Wilkinson (11)**
**Dunfermline High School**

# My Holiday

Last year I went on holiday to Spain. I stayed
in a really nice hotel. I went to a big theme park
which had lots of roller coasters. On the last day I
went to Barcelona. The next day I went home.
I had a really good time in Spain.

**Anton Zarzoso (1)**
**Falkland House School**

# Are We Alone

One ordinary night I was coming back from my friend's house after watching the football game. When I was driving home I saw a weird object in the sky. It was silvery-black and glowing. I started to wonder, are we alone?

## Joshua Gracie (14)
**Falkland House School**

# The Heavy Wooden Door

I rushed through the castle halls. They all looked the same. Soon I found myself in a dark, mysterious, round room with a heavy wooden door. My heart was pounding as I stood wondering what was behind the heavy door. I tried the heavy door, but it was too late …

**Jonathan Burke (12)**
**Falkland House School**

# The Ghost Truck

The monster truck show came to town. I went to see it. The noise was incredible. Over the noise I heard a cry. You could not see anything. A truck roared straight towards me. I cringed, an icy blast passed through me … my blood froze.

**Steven Barrett (14)**
**Falkland House School**

# The Unforgettable Night

One night these two boys went on a camping
trip they will never forget. They were in dark, creepy
woods as happy as Larry, when suddenly they heard
something, something scary. They went outside,
then suddenly, mysteriously, fell dead.
You never know what could be lurking
in the creepy woods.

**Oliver Costigan (10)**
**Falkland House School**

# Revenge

I saw my wee cousin totally stoned.
I asked him where he got the drugs and he
said this drug dealer. I plotted revenge.
I met him in the pub. I gave him a lethal
cocktail and watched him die in agony.
I died laughing.

**Ross Hogg (14)**
**Falkland House School**

# One Dark Night

It was a dark, isolated place. Jim didn't know if he would make it through the night. He heard a noise, so he turned and ran towards the door. He opened it, but it was a dead end. Would he survive the nightmare?

**Ryan Brotherston (13)**
**Falkland House School**

# The Photographers

There were two boys called Ross and Liam.
They were model photographers for the Scottish
Gallery, also magazine producers. They earned a lot
of money for their jobs. It was a fun job, they had
been doing it for ten years. The camera flashed,
they became negative forever!

**Liam Louden (14)**
**Falkland House School**

# Surprise!

It looked at me with a smile. 'Link's the name,' it said.
'My name's Sophie.'
And with that it turned and fluttered its wings in my
face and was gone. What had I just rescued?
I couldn't believe my eyes!

**Amy Graham (13)**
**Kirkland High School & Community College**

# Crash!

I close the door behind me and walk along
the street to the bus stop. I cross the road to check
the timetable. There is a half hour wait.
The bus comes. I sit at the back and phone Dad.
The bus goes round the roundabout … *boom!*

### Steven Robertson (13)
**Kirkland High School & Community College**

# Le Petit Explosif

Last lesson of the day - French.
Tapping my pencil with boredom, it slipped
from my hand and hit the floor with a thud. The
teacher stood up and looked annoyed. She stretched
out her arm and bent over. *Parp!* Laughter filled the
room. Now it wasn't so boring!

**Alex Adams (13)**
**Kirkland High School & Community College**

61

# Drip, Drip, Drip

Morgan enters her flat. She has three roommates, but where are they? She hears dripping, *drip, drip, drip*. *Water or blood?* She thinks. A shiver goes down her spine. She checks the flat for her roommates. She switches on the lights. 'Surprise!'

**Robbie Leitch (13)**
**Kirkland High School & Community College**

62

# Me, Myself And I

Everywhere I go I am alone. At school, at home, when I go out. Even when I'm in a shop, everyone runs away. I don't know why. I think to myself, *do I smell?* But I don't. I still don't know why I'm alone.

**Kelsey Wilson (13)**
**Kirkland High School & Community College**

# The Snowman

I awoke. It was snowing. I quickly dressed. I shoved on wellies and ran outside. I made a snowman. Once finished, I gathered a hat, scarf and a carrot for him. The sun shone. Mum called me in for breakfast. I opened the door. Where was he?

**Nicola England (13)**
**Kirkland High School & Community College**

# Urial's Last Stand

The attack came in surges. Urial ducked and parried as bayonets came flying at him. He dived left as one of the heretics shot at him. He lunged forward, pushing his sword into the man's gut. Blood sprayed and as Urial looked around, he realised the battle was already over.

**Ross Macfarlane (13)**
**Kirkland High School & Community College**

# The Rag Doll

Lucy Williams' doll was called Becki.
She loved Becki lots and so did Lucy's friend, Emily.
One day, Emily came to Lucy's for tea, but was
that all Emily came for because when Lucy woke
up the next morning, Becki was gone.
Had Emily taken Becki?

## Sarah Bradley (13)
**Kirkland High School & Community College**

# House 666

*Weird!* I thought as I walked through the distant halls of the house. Strange, unreal things have happened here. Sometimes I can hear the sound of feet on the floor above me; the sound of bodies being dragged below me. I can hear the clock going *tick, tick, tick … tock.*

**Steven Welsh (12)**
**Kirkland High School & Community College**

67

# It's A Doggy Dog World Out There

Cody was walking down the street.
He felt weird. He felt warm, fluffy; a sudden hate
for cats and a desire to chew shoes. Then he saw
Suzy and went to see her, but she turned around
and shouted, 'Back off you spooky dog!'

**Bailfie Blount (13)**
**Kirkland High School & Community College**

68

# In The Dark

Sitting alone. Dark room. Don't like the feeling.
*Creak, creak, eee-eee-eeer.*
*'Argh!'* What happened? I sat alone, nowhere
to go and then … I woke up! Just a dream!

**Niall Anderson (13)**
**Kirkland High School & Community College**

# The Sundae

The chocolate cascades down the side
of an ice cream cone so quickly that you'd think
it had somewhere to go! It drowns out the other
flavours attempting to grace a woman's siren-red lips.
The vanilla struggles to melt but this day,
Ben and Jerry's freezer is icy.

**Flora Ogilvy (13)**
**St Leonard's School, St Andrews**

# Killed In The Accident

The street, the tree, we slipped - *crash!*
A loud noise, shaking, darkness, then suddenly
light, fire. I saw her lying in front of me, blood
everywhere, her eyes without light, empty. Mine full
of tears, sadness. I lost her. She was dead. Killed
in the accident, never coming back again.

**Dominique Haferkamp (15)**
**St Leonard's School, St Andrews**

71

# Midnight Graves

The night was black, the stars hidden in the clouds.
He was digging, digging. Sweat dripped down his face.
All the time he was digging, he heard her screams
in his head. 'Please, no, I beg of you, spare me!'
Just as he placed her in the grave, he fell …

**Lily Watts (13)**
**St Leonard's School, St Andrews**

# The Daunting Acquaintance

Approaching the station. Her phone rang.
It was the boy. She could hear the icy tone,
'I can't talk to you anymore. It's too dangerous.'
'Why? Are the stories true?'
'Please, just trust me.'
'But …'
A gun sounded. She turned around.
The figure in the duffel coat darted away.

**Rebecca Taylor (13)**
**St Leonard's School, St Andrews**

# On The Road

'Stop!' The carriage lurched and halted.
'Get out! Hands up!' the voice said. I obeyed,
chin held high. Highwaymen. There were two,
but I was prepared. I struck the first over the head.
He collapsed. I held my pistol to the other's temple.
'Elizabeth ...' he stammered.
It was my brother.

**Olivia Coffison-Owen (13)**
**St Leonard's School, St Andrews**

74

# Pursuit

The wind whistled and groaned, rain pelted the saturated ground. On he ran, heedless of the storm. Lightning lit the moor. He glimpsed sanctuary ahead. For the unholy thing couldn't enter the church … could it? Another stride and he was sinking. Mud swiftly engulfed him. Oh God, not the mire …

**Grace Coffison-Owen (13)**
**St Leonard's School, St Andrews**

# The Golden Sword

Walking along the riverbank, whistling to myself. Birds tweeting, wind rustling through my hair. Minding my own business. *Clunk!* My foot struck something wooden. It's a sword and a golden one at that! I rushed back to my parents shouting. My parents always told me not to make up stories.

**Jamie Hartley (13)**
**St Leonard's School, St Andrews**

# The Commuter

A cold winter's morning. London just awaking.
Late commuter running. He misses the train. Gets
a quick coffee and sits reading paper. Hops on the
bus. Awoken by speaker, 'Piccadilly Circus.' He
scrambles off. Beckons a taxi. 'To the bank, fast!'
Pays good tip. Runs to desk …
'Late again! Fired!'

**Claudia Beasley (13)**
**St Leonard's School, St Andrews**

# That Night

Silent. Unmoving. A village at night. I walked,
hands in my pockets, with only the orange glow
of the streetlights for company. Then a scream.
I stopped, confused. A movement behind me.
I looked round, terrified. A hollow voice …
'Trick or treat?'
It was Hallowe'en.

**Callum Robertson (13)**
**St Leonard's School, St Andrews**

# The Best Man

I was going to miss the wedding. I ran down the dirty stone steps faster and faster, my suitcase bumping along behind. I could hear the train pulling into the station. The conductor was calling out, 'All aboard!' The train departed. I arrived on the platform. 'Darn it!'

**Olivia Cassidy (13)**
**St Leonard's School, St Andrews**

# The Unexpected Miracle

Dad drove to the hospital. Uncharacteristically,
he stopped for a bearded hitchhiker who got
into the back seat. 'Have you found Jesus?'
'No,' my dad replied.
On arrival at the hospital, my father noticed
the hitchhiker gone, his seatbelt still fastened.
'Your tumour's disappeared,' the oncologist
announced. 'It's a miracle!'

**Natalie Degroot (13)**
**St Leonard's School, St Andrews**

# The Deserving Beggar

He had been walking for days.
He was tired and hungry. Now he reached London.
'Spare a penny.'
A beautiful woman swept him off his feet.
'Come with me.'
They walked promptly through the alleyways.
Never taking his gaze away from her,
afraid he would lose her forever.

**Anna Rolland (13)**
**St Leonard's School, St Andrews**

# The Family Business

I arrived at the meeting. I sat down next to
him. I ordered food and we discussed business,
but I didn't listen to one word. I focussed on the job.
As planned, it was in the restroom. I got up. I came
back. I sat down. I pulled the trigger.

### Ian Redford (15)
**St Leonard's School, St Andrews**

# The Germ

I was inhaled on a dark and cold winter's morning. Into the lungs I swirled like a tornado before entering the bloodstream. I was killing him as I multiplied uncontrollably, flowing round his system. I didn't mean to take his life, he inhaled me from the air - I, the germ.

**Ewan Anderson (12)**
**St Leonard's School, St Andrews**

# We're All Human

I'm cold. Waiting to go into battle.
The English think we're horrible, but we're not.
We just do what we're told. We don't want to kill
them. I see them now, a huge mob approaching.
They've got guns. Please let this end soon, because
although we disagree, we're all human.

**Claire Marston (11)**
**St Leonard's School, St Andrews**

# Ophelia's Lake

She turns, mad. She walks, her sadness echoes.
Mad with grief. She walks up a hill, seeing the lake
below she smiles. She steps. Wind billows through
her hair. She plunges into the deep. She's drowning.
Ophelia is no more. Hamlet is distraught.
It happened because he killed her father.

**Miriam Balfour (12)**
**St Leonard's School, St Andrews**

# Untitled

Catherine walked down the dark and lonely tunnel. It was quiet. Suddenly, she heard a rustling noise behind her. She turned around. Nothing was there. She walked on. Appearing out of nowhere, someone jumped out of a small doorway. She tried to run. That night she was never seen again.

**Mikayla Head (12)**
**St Leonard's School, St Andrews**

# The Witch

The cat's green eyes looked around.
It was a witch. I stood stock still. The witch
turned, looking me straight in the eyes, but I was
gone. I dodged through every single street, trying
to escape her icy grasp. It was impossible.
After that night, I was never seen again.

**Lauren Goadby (11)**
**St Leonard's School, St Andrews**

87

# The Scream

It was that day. She was at home, alone. She heard
a voice. 'I can see you,' it hissed. She jumped up and
ran to the door. 'Don't try and escape, I will get you.'
This time she looked up. It was there.
*Argh!* Was the last sound anyone heard.

**Charlotte Fitton (12)**
**St Leonard's School, St Andrews**

# The Assassin

My hand flickered, watching my prey slowly
sauntering down the street. Memories of betrayal
circled and soared in my head like eagles in flight.
Through the crosshairs, cold, dark eyes blankly stare.
Now in my sights, black cross hovering over his face.
My fingers squeeze. An explosion of red …

**Michael Overend  (13)**
**St Leonard's School, St Andrews**

89

# A Race Against Time

Her footsteps quickened as she raced along the darkened alley. The wind whistled and litter blew across her path. Would she reach the end of the alley in time? The footsteps behind were catching up; her heart pounded. She turned the corner. But what was waiting for her?

**Lauren Sandeman (14)**
**St Leonard's School, St Andrews**

# Untitled

I walk, head shielded low. Wounding words, abuse hurled hard. Did I deserve this? Try to ignore the pain, the snatching spite. Leaving me empty, a dark void. The teacher, oblivious, parents unaware. Life losing all hope, all promise. This world not for me. I jump. Everything stops, dead.

**Liam Deboys  (15)**
**St Leonard's School, St Andrews**

# The Roller Coaster

Sitting, waiting, tension building.
Comrade close beside. A woman joins; trio
formed. Countdown, adrenalin rising. Blast-off.
Hurtling round loops and vortex, corkscrews and
banks. The world flashes past, blurred. Shooting stars
fly, streaks of light. We slow down, back to Earth.
I turn round, smile faltering. Comrade is gone.

**Rebecca Mansbridge (14)**
**St Leonard's School, St Andrews**

# Trapped

The light dimmed, the silence was deadly.
Foot after foot, I ran through the darkness. The fog
thickened, I could hear my breathing getting faster.
All was quiet, until suddenly I heard voices coming
from all around, footsteps from all directions, my
time was up. There was no way out!

**Annabel Zajicek (13)**
**St Leonard's School, St Andrews**

# Decision Time

The air still and dry. My comrades worn and down. Slowly they emerged over the brow of the hill, armed to the teeth and spirits high. We stood no chance, not a hope in hell. Should we fight our hearts out and die, or run? What were we to do?

**Joseph Levett  (15)**
**St Leonard's School, St Andrews**

# Kidnapped

I stared, watery eyed, at his dry, flaking hands,
his bashed, yellow nails as he tightly wound
the broad, rigid rope around my fragile body.
I winced with pain. He tugged the rope.
My insides compressed. I struggled. I lost.

**Fiona Baird (13)**
St Leonard's School, St Andrews

# Waterfall

There it was, the end of the waterfall and
surely my life. There was simply no way of escape.
I could hear my heart pumping faster every second.
No! Down I went, plummeting to a watery death.
I looked down. Nearly there. *Splash!*
Then I woke up from my sleep.

**Josh Jamieson (14)**
**St Leonard's School, St Andrews**

# Hurricane

It started as a gust of wind, then it built up
and up, rampaging through cities in one straight line.
House after house, street after street, car after car.
Moscow to Strasburg, then China to Taiwan.
Then it reached the ocean and was gone forever.

**Ged Rutherford (13)**
**St Leonard's School, St Andrews**

# Oh No!

Last night I had a nightmare. I called out in my sleep,
'Where is everybody? I want my friends!'
Finally, morning came.
'Max!' a voice called.
I opened one eye and saw Vanessa walking towards
me, shaking a box. 'Breakfast time!'
'Oh no, not doggie bites again!'

**Darya Vinogradov-Wouters (12)**
**St Leonard's School, St Andrews**

# Sniff

Snuffles and ruffles. Lots of footsteps.
I grew more scared. A slow creak and the door
slammed open. More small, padding footsteps.
I steadied my breath and pretended I was sleeping.
'Get her,' I heard.
My dog, Molly, jumped up and licked my face. Ugh!
Disgusting!

**Aime Affan (12)**
**Woodmill High School**

99

# Untitled

He stared into her eyes and she stared back.
It was love at first sight, it had to be. He then put
his glasses back on and his eyes came into focus. He
discovered he was staring at the ugliest witch ever!

## Emma Archer (13)
### Woodmill High School

# Horror Story

I was walking through the dark woods alone.
The squirrels were shaking the trees, which made
it scary. Suddenly, I saw bright, gleaming eyes staring
at me. I wondered what it was, so I started running.
I heard flapping behind me. It was following me.
It was a freaky bat!

**Sophie Bafsiffie  (12)**
**Woodmill High School**

lol

# The Black Life

It was coming fast, faster than expected.
It was black and fast, not a nice combination.
I was white with anxiety. Time was going slowly,
too slowly. People were watching me. Just slowly
losing my reputation. I was dreading this day.
My picture and my life were ruined.

**Christopher Bogie (12)**
**Woodmill High School**

# A Day In The Life Of A Dog

A day in the life of a dog is a very boring one indeed.
He lies on the floor and watches TV, eating the
leftover food. When his owner returns his stomach
churns as 'walkies' is called from afar.

## Kelly Boniface (13)
### Woodmill High School

# The Gates Of Hell

The gates of Hell opened with a creak. It was horrible. Swarms of red imps were flying everywhere, while a large shadow came slowly from the fiery gates. The gates closed with a loud slam. The beast was out!

**Jonathan Cameron (13)**
**Woodmill High School**

# Old Things

The room was quiet, the only sound
was the groaning of the thing, limping towards me.
Sweat ran down my back, chilling me to the bone in
this dark place. I stared wide-eyed, not believing this
was real. The thing stopped. I sighed, relieved.
It was only my grandad!

**Nicole Chappell (12)**
**Woodmill High School**

# The Crowd

We were stumbling up the hill, jostled by big crowds.
We finally got there. Suddenly, people started
screaming, shouting and roaring. We had missed
the first goal. Rangers one, Celtic nil.

**Tiffany Concannon (13)**
**Woodmill High School**

# Triumphant

Clutching Fred the ted, I slowly lifted my foot onto the cold, bare mountain. The path seemed endless, winding itself round the wall. *Eeek!* I jumped, sprinting forward. I ran to the top. Holding Fred high, I stood proud. I had climbed the hall stairs.

**Megan Doran (12)**
**Woodmill High School**

# Lowdown

I've got the lowdown on this guy: name, address,
age - it's all here. I've got all his details. Good …
he's our contest winner.

**Aaron Dougan (14)**
**Woodmill High School**

# Kidnapped!

Me and my friends were walking along
the road when a man stepped out and told us
we had won a million pounds. He said he would
take us to claim it. I said no, but my friend went.
Three weeks they've been searching
and still no sign of her!

**Carla Dow (13)**
**Woodmill High School**

# Untitled

The clock chimed twelve o'clock.
'I have to go,' said Cinderella.
'Why?' asked Prince Charming.
'Coronation Street's on.'

**Hannah Feff (12)**
**Woodmill High School**

# The Death Of A Friend

The dark figure stood over a limp body,
a knife held loosely in his bloodstained hand. What
had he done? Why had he killed his best friend?
He remembered the fierce argument the morning
before, how his friend had tormented him. He
rammed the knife into him and walked away.

**Benjamin Fofan (13)**
**Woodmill High School**

# Car Chase

I was driving fast, trying to get away from them. I drifted around the next corner, dodging around other drivers, but a van came out of nowhere. I hit it and they caught me. The screen went blank … game over.

## Michael Henderson (13)
### Woodmill High School

# Untitled

*Vroom, vroom!* We're off! Number 10 has the lead. Oh no, now it's 42. The finish line is in sight and 10 wins. 'Damn! He beats me every time!' said Dad.

## Daniel Jones (12)
### Woodmill High School

# Untitled

One team had just scored. The fans had gone mental!
Both sides of supporters cheering on their favourite
teams. The same team scored again. The crowd
went wild, one half celebrating and the other half
sobbing with their hopes destroyed.
This wasn't just a match, it was a cup final!

**Ryan Kay (13)**
**Woodmill High School**

# Untitled

In a huge, dark galaxy, there was a
creepy planet and on the creepy planet was a scary
country, and in that scary country was an abandoned
town, and in the abandoned town was a ghostly
house, and in that ghostly house was an extremely
freaky, very dangerous and rare …

**Kerry Keiſſoh (13)**
**Woodmill High School**

# The Epic Journey

Sweat travelled down my forehead.
My arms could hardly lift off the ground. I couldn't
go on. Someone told me I could make it. I made one
final lunge and grabbed it. Then I leapt onto the
sofa and changed the channel.

**Christopher Leslie (11)**
**Woodmill High School**

116

# Penalty

I stood up to the ball, looked ahead of me. Nothing but the fresh breeze in my face. I was sweating and the nerves were getting to me. Nothing but two sticks either side of a fat boy with sweaty hair and gloves in front. The whistle sounded. *Goal!*

## Stewart McDonald (12)
### Woodmill High School

# Tommy The Warrior

The trees towered high above, the sounds
of nature all around. It was Tommy in the jungle,
alone. He was triumphant as he cut through the
leaves. He was a warrior, here in the Amazon.
The sun broke through, his mum was there!
'Come in, Tommy, tea's on the table.'

### Kendra McPherson (12)
**Woodmill High School**

# Presence

They were hovering around me, but then suddenly, they started to go round in circles getting dizzy and uncontrollable. I just couldn't stay still. Then one of them came swooping down hard and fast. That's when everything went blank.

**Kirsty-Marie Moran (13)**
**Woodmill High School**

# Nessie

As we sat on the little wooden boat,
it began to bob. Then a giant shadow was cast
under the boat. We didn't know what it was.
*Was it a whale? Couldn't be,* I thought.
Then a huge, green, Jurassic-looking
creature jumped out of the loch.
'Was that Nessie?'

**Lauren Queen (13)**
**Woodmill High School**

# Winter Fright

Every corner she turned she saw more witches and skeletons. She couldn't get away from them. She went to every house she could, but half of them didn't even open the door, though she knew they were in. She looked in her bag. It was practically empty!
'I hate Hallowe'en!'

**Nisha Rach (13)**
**Woodmill High School**

121

# Lost At Sea?

It was a sunny day. My friend and I were
at the beach joking around. We went into the
sea to cool off. After a while I came out to dry off.
Lucy said she would be out in five minutes …
I'm still waiting.

**Chlöe Reiffy (13)**
**Woodmill High School**

# Stuck

I was walking up the stairs, heading for my room when I felt this feeling. It was my stomach. I ran faster and faster. I reached my destiny - the toilet. I pulled down my pants and sat on the pan, but when I was done, I was stuck.

**Tomas Mark Sibbald (12)**
**Woodmill High School**

# The Bombs

'They're coming!'
*Boom! Boom!* The bombs are dropping and the
deafening bombs blowing up are making me scream.
'No Jake, don't go out there, you'll die. Jake, *nooo!'*
Oh no! Who taped over my movie
with the Teletubbies?
'Declan!'

### Conor Smith (12)
**Woodmill High School**

# Murder Of A Friend

I crept through the front door and quietly closed it behind me. The hall was brightly lit and I could see the bedroom door. I crept over and opened it. I saw him sleeping, open-mouthed. Anger flashed through me as I plunged my dagger into his heart of stone.

**Vicky Sparling (13)**
**Woodmill High School**

# Little Green Man

'Get the gun!'
A voice came from nowhere. I was shaking. I'd never been in a situation like this. There was a little green man walking in the door. I grabbed a gun. My little brother got soaked right through, covered in green paint.

**Craig Stephen (12)**
**Woodmill High School**

# The Three Little Pigs

'I'll huff and I'll puff and I'll blow your house down.'
'But why? Wouldn't you prefer to
share my Sunday roast instead?'
He came in. I ran out the back door.
He was so angry. He huffed and he puffed
and he blew my house down!

**Cameron Tasker (12)**
**Woodmill High School**

# Untitled

My face is hidden by a hood as I attempt the most dangerous feat ever. My hand is shaking as I hold the handle of my dagger. He walks past. I get ready. I jump out, plunging the dagger into his back. He falls to the ground. Tyranny is dead.

**Sean Tetsaff (13)**
**Woodmill High School**

# Untitled

Behind the tree, hiding. It was coming closer.
Heart beating, I could hear its footsteps. I was
shivering with horror. It came. No time to run.
'Ha, ha! You're it!'

**Fearghas Urquhart (11)**
**Woodmill High School**

# Hero

One day I was walking along the road.
I turned my head and saw a girl lying on the road.
Suddenly, I saw a lorry speeding. I grabbed the girl.
I heard brakes screeching.
Whoa, made it! I was a hero!

**Samantha McDonald (12)**
**Woodmill High School**

# The House

The door opened! They walked inside. The walls covered in cobwebs. They struggled upstairs. They heard a noise, it was the police. They ran to the front door, but it was locked. They turned round. There was a man with a gun …

## Tony McAulay (14)
### Woodmill High School

# My Reflection

As I saw my reflection in the mirror, I noticed I moved, but I didn't. My reflection was moving on its own. I screamed and ran. With a bang, I found myself lying on my bedroom floor. I looked and saw myself again and my reflection was never the same ...

**Ashleigh McAndrew (12)**
**Woodmill High School**

# The Night Without Mum

I was sitting, cold, stiff. It was dark and I was waiting for my mum to come home. The phone rang. No one was there. It rang again, still no answer. The doorbell rang. I slowly walked towards the door. Someone spoke …
It was Mum! I was so relieved.

**Gemma Lane  (13)**
**Woodmill High School**

# The Stormy Night

On the stormy night I was lying in bed. Something was tapping the window. I dared not move. The tapping got louder, scraping on the window, making a shiver go down my spine. I slowly went up to the window, quickly opened the curtain …
It was the tree!

**Adam Giffen (13)**
**Woodmill High School**

# In The Dark

*Ring, ring!* The doorbell. 'Argh! What do I do?'
I looked out the window. I saw a scary, dark figure
at the door. I lay down on the floor, not sure what
to do. I looked out of the corner of my eye.
I saw the Tesco van.

## Sara Eydmann (12)
### Woodmill High School

# Trapped

I was running down the street, being
chased by the living dead. They were everywhere!
My instinct told me to run!
I ran down an alleyway. Damn! Trapped like a mouse.
They were everywhere. One bullet left. I panicked.
The words flashed up on the screen - game over!

## Maddie Coussens (13)
**Woodmill High School**

# Untitled

As I sat on the stone-cold bench, paralysed with fear, I chanced a look at the tall man standing behind me and my friend. We looked at each other terrified, wondering what would happen next. My friend stood up, against the man's orders. *Bang!* My friend was gone, forever.

**Lauren Buchanan (13)**
**Woodmill High School**

# The Statue

I said, 'Hello sir, are you okay?' He didn't move a muscle, not even a blink. My heart pounded like drums. I ran to my mum and told her. She said, 'Oh no, that's a statue looking like a man.' But when we went back through, he wasn't there!

**Robyn Affan (13)**
**Woodmill High School**

# Information

We hope you have enjoyed reading this book - and that you will continue to enjoy it in the coming years.

If you like reading and writing, drop us a line or give us a call and we'll send you a free information pack. Alternatively visit our website at www.youngwriters.co.uk

Write to:
Young Writers Information,
Remus House,
Coltsfoot Drive,
Peterborough,
PE2 9JX
Tel: (01733) 890066
Email: youngwriters@forwardpress.co.uk